I Hope Your Dreams Are Sweet

Written By
Steppie Morris

Illustrated By
Elysse Hopkins

To my Angel, who inspires me and is such a great example! And
to all my angels that I have been privileged to tuck into bed at
night. It's an honor to be your mom! ~ SM

LAWLEY
PUBLISHING

This edition first published in 2021
by Lawley Publishing,
a division of Lawley Enterprises LLC.

Text Copyright © 2021 by Steppie Morris
Illustration Copyright © 2021 by Elysse Hopkins
All Rights Reserved

Lawley Publishing
70 S. Val Vista Dr. #A3 #188
Gilbert, Az. 85296
www.LawleyPublishing.com

But bedtime has arrived.
I see your drooping eyes.

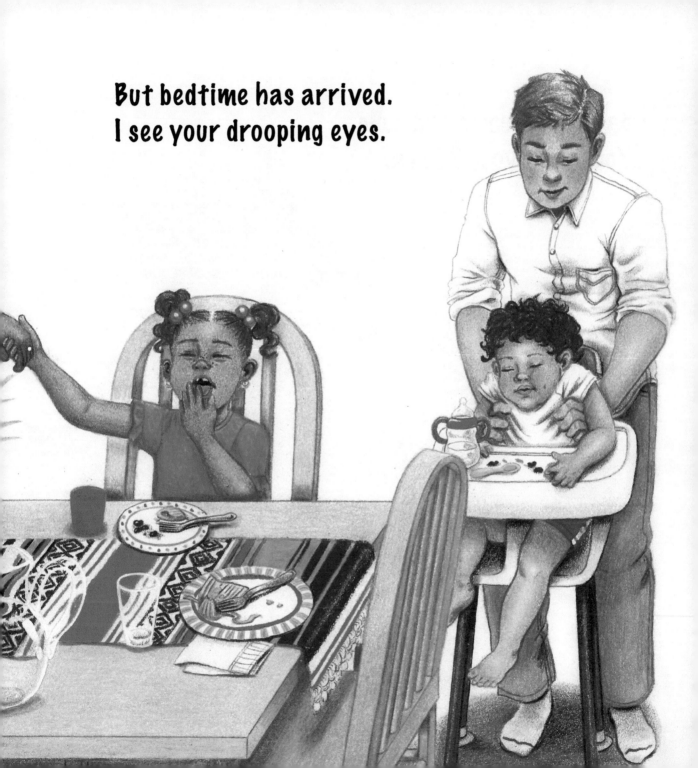

Baths have come and gone.
You've put your PJs on.

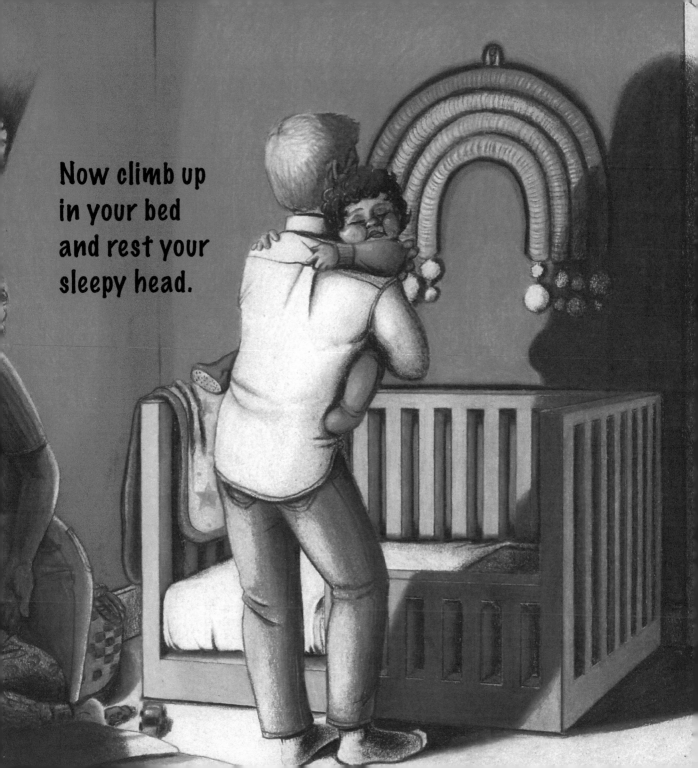

Now climb up in your bed and rest your sleepy head.

I hope your dreams are sweet.

No monsters shall you meet.

I've faith
you'll get
good rest

so you
can be
your best,

and grow
up big and
strong,

find joy
your whole
life long.

And when push
comes to shove,

For now, close tired eyes.
The night will surely fly.
Another day will dawn,
and life will still rush on.

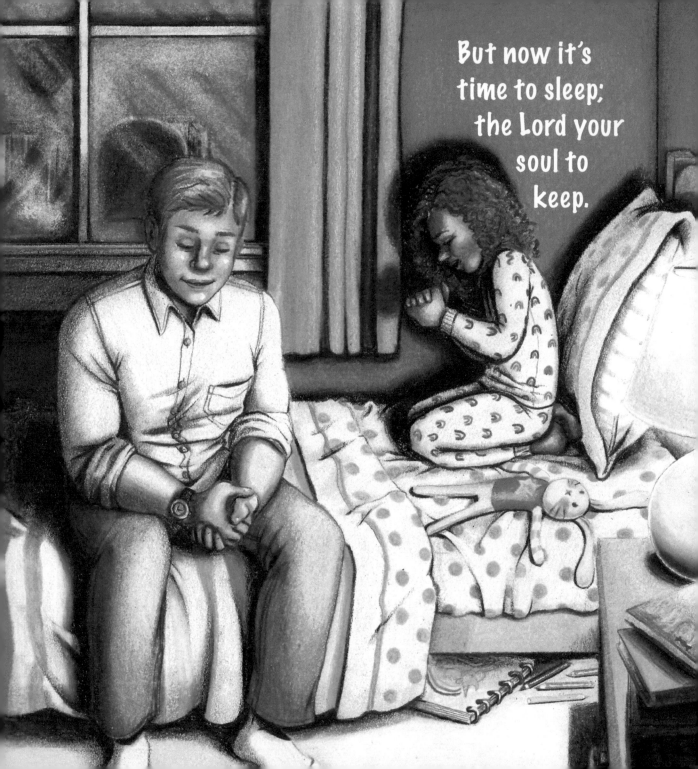

A hug and
one last kiss,
the ones I
will not miss.

I'll tuck the sheet up tight
and turn on your night light.

Bedtime Tip

READ

BEDTIME

STORIES!!

Want more insightful, empowering, fun children's books?

For more books parents can trust and kids will love, visit us at

www.lawleypublishing.com

For updates and info on New Releases follow us at

lawleypublishing

@kidsbookswithheart

LAWLEY
PUBLISHING

Stephanie gained her nickname, Steppie Dance, from her brother because she's a dancer, and he's just plain crazy! She is happiest surrounded by her family and has loved raising her five kids with a bedtime story nearly every night (even when they were teens—shhh, don't tell)! When not reading, she can be found writing, cooking, in a yoga pose, or sneaking an extra chocolate chip cookie—with milk, of course.

Elysse is a wife and a new mommy to a little boy. Illustrating children's books has been a life dream of hers since she was young, and the message in this book has found resonance in her heart as she has recently been learning what it means to be a mother. She loves snuggling her baby and holding him close and cherishing these precious moments, even if the days are wild.

CPSIA information can be obtained
at www.ICGtesting.com
Printed in the USA
BVHW021203300821
615417BV00022B/645